HOW DO YOU HIDE A MONSTER?

by Virginia Kahl

Charles Scribner's Sons   New York

Printed in the United States of America/SBN 684-12318-5 (cloth)/SBN 684-13508-6 (paper)
Library of Congress Catalog Card Number 73-143926/ 1 3 5 7 9 M/P 10 8 6 4 2

Off in the mountains, beyond a wood,
Near a deep dark lake, a village stood.
It stood for years and it stands today,
Hidden and secret and far away.
Few strangers ventured beyond the wood
To the hidden spot where the village stood.
Even today, few undertake
To find their way to the deep dark lake.

The forest is filled with the finest of fowl
From the tiniest wren to a large old owl.
On the mountaintop there are beasts galore,
From the littlest mole to an enormous boar.

And the lake has fish; but its principal feature
Is Phinney, a cheerful kindly creature.

He paddles and dives to the watery caves
Where succulent plants grow beneath the waves.
He's lived there forever, so it appears,
For he's been there for years and years and years.

And everyone says, "He's a cheerful fellow,
With his beautiful body of greeny-yellow.
Such a friendly beast, and he seems to care:
If ever we need him, he's always there.
If fishermen fear that they've lost their way,
Old Phinney will see that they do not stray.
If a child paddles off when he's out for a swim,
Old Phinney keeps watch and takes care of him.
We never need worry when Phinney's about.
He's the rare kind of friend we can't do without."

So they all were happy until the day
That a letter arrived from far away.
It said,
"Lock your doors and tread with care;
There's a fearful, frightful beast out there.
A traveler lost near your lake and wood
Has sighted a monster (and that's not good!)"

"A monster! How dreadful!" the people cried.
"We're lucky that Phinney is on our side.
When we find the monster and sound alarm,
He'll see that none of us comes to harm.
He'll fight and conquer that dreaded beast
Or frighten him off, at the very least.

But how does a frightful monster look?
Can we recognize him without a book?

Is he splay-footed?
Snub-nosed?
Spiky-eared?

Shaggy or bearded or very weird?

Like a monstrous bird?

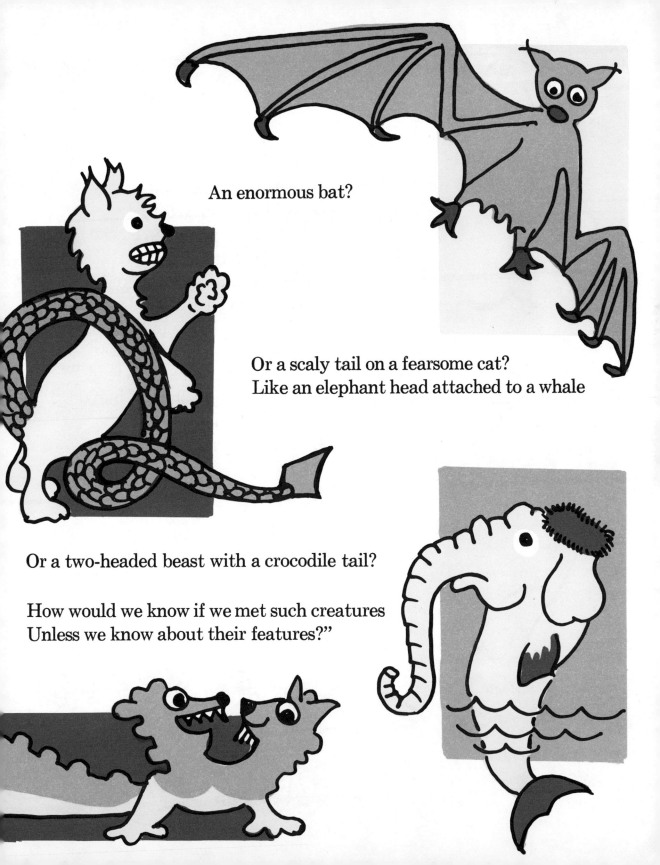

An enormous bat?

Or a scaly tail on a fearsome cat?
Like an elephant head attached to a whale

Or a two-headed beast with a crocodile tail?

How would we know if we met such creatures
Unless we know about their features?"

The message told what the man had seen:
An enormous beast of yellowy-green,
With a sinuous neck and a small fierce head
That had no hair, but had horns instead.
It had two fangs that were sharp and long
And a jaw that seemed to be cruel and strong
And a body that stretched half a mile, at least,
All shiny and glowing—a fearsome beast!
"But never you fear," the townspeople read.
"We'll capture the beast, or we'll shoot him dead.
We're sending some men to investigate,
For this is a problem that cannot wait."

The townspeople gasped and remarked, "We fear
That letter describes our Phinney dear.
He isn't fearful; he isn't frightful;
He's not a monster; he's too delightful."
And they looked toward the lake, where they could see
Old Phinney splashing happily.
Not very much of him could be seen
Except his head of yellowy-green,
And his long white fangs and his powerful jaw
Were just about all that the townsfolk saw.
And everyone cried, "There's been an error;
That beast is never a cause for terror.
He'd never harm us; he's kind and true.
We must protect him; what shall we do?"
At last they announced, after due reflection,
"We'll send the men off in the wrong direction."

The very next day some men came through
Professors and hunters and soldiers, too.
They carried weapons,
    consulted books,
To be sure they'd know
    how a monster looks.

They announced, "Tonight we're going to take
Our weapons down to the deep dark lake.
We'll surely capture the monster there;
That's probably where he has his lair."

"No!" cried the townsfolk. "That's no good.
He's bound to be in the deep dark wood."

That night they crept into the wood
And waited as quietly as they could,
Till one of the hunters sneezed a sneeze
That ruffled the leaves on the nearest trees.
From high above them came eerie cries;
They saw two balefully blinking eyes.
The men cried, "Monster!" and shivered with fear.
"We'll shoot him, now that we've trapped him here."
But the townsfolk said, "Wait till it's light.
You can't shoot straight on such a night."

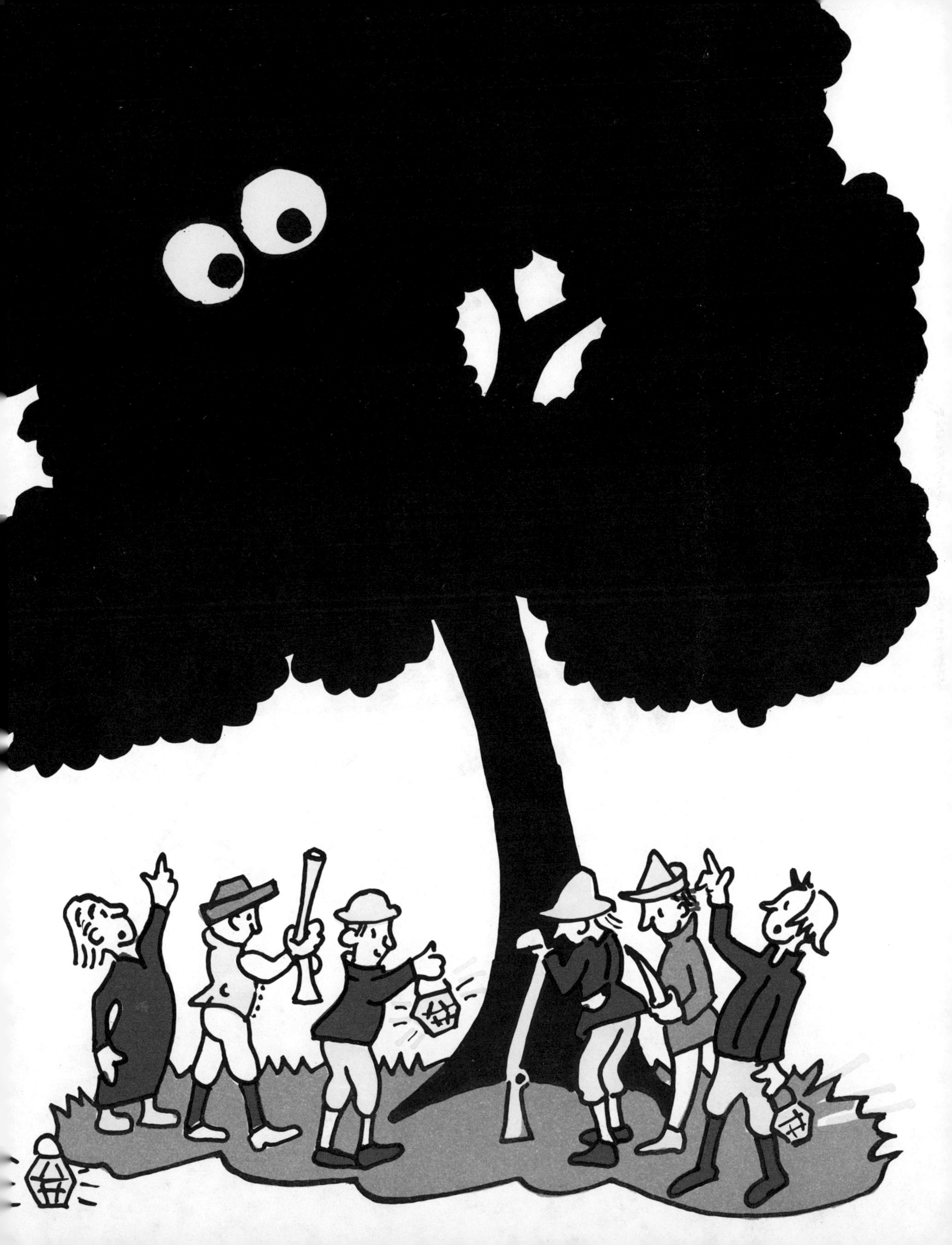

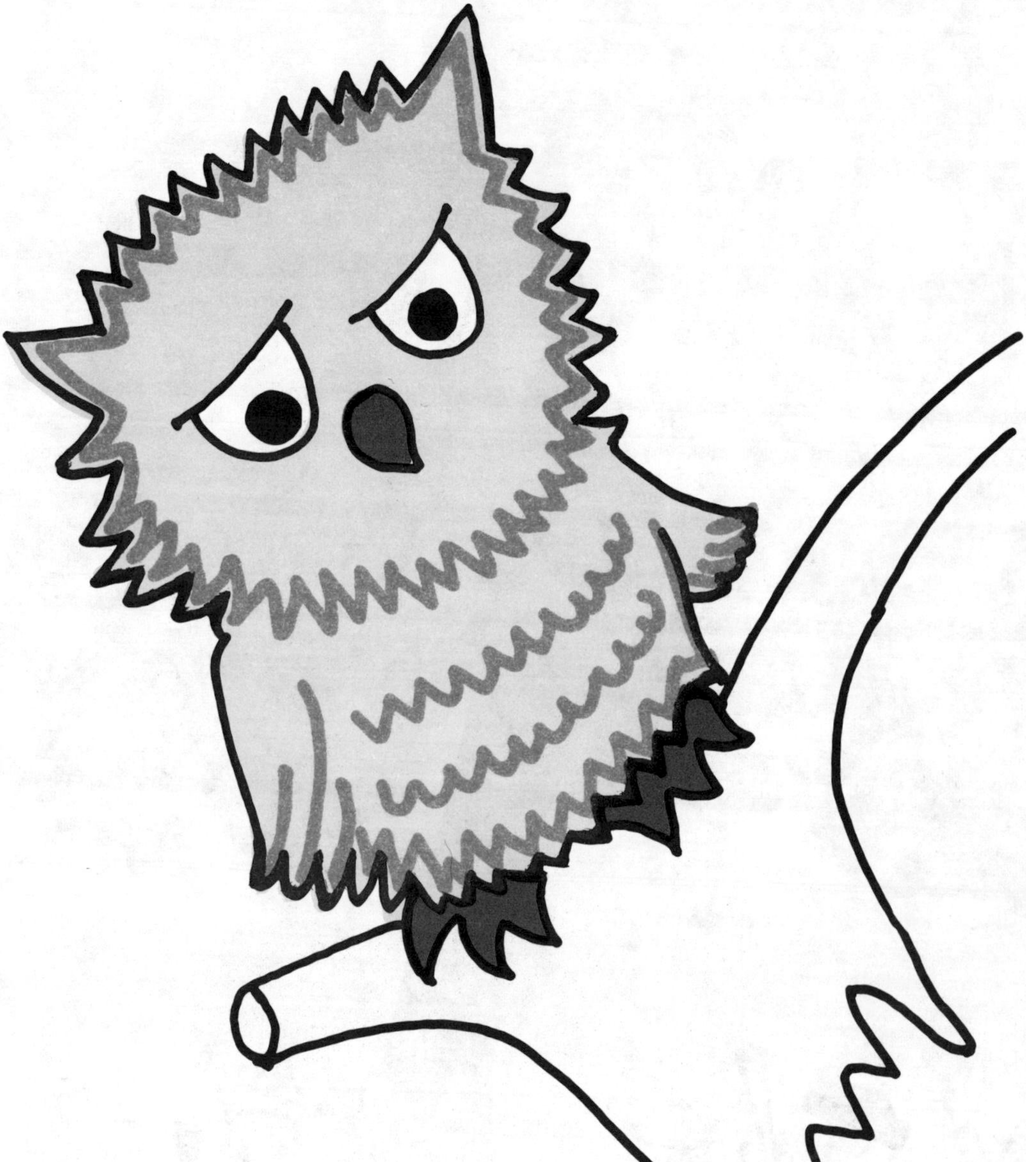

At dawn the men set up a howl.
"It's just a big old sleepy owl!
It's a monster we want, not an owl in his nest.
Let's go back to the inn and get a good rest."

The second night they said, "We'll take
Our weapons to the deep dark lake.
That's where the monster lurks, we know.
When evening comes, then, off we'll go!"

Again, the townsfolk cried, "No! No!
That's not the place for you to go.
On the mountain we've heard a fearful sound;
That's where a monster's to be found.
There's a thicket there that's dark and scary
Where something lives that's huge and hairy."

That night the men went off to seek
The monster on the mountain peak.
When they reached the thicket, they heard a shuffle,
And a gurgle-y, sniffle-y sort of snuffle
That made their blood run cold as ice
(And that's a feeling that isn't nice).

"The cannon!" they cried. "We'll shoot the beast,
Or chase him away, at the very least."
But the townspeople said, "Wait till it's dawn.
He'll still be here; he won't be gone."

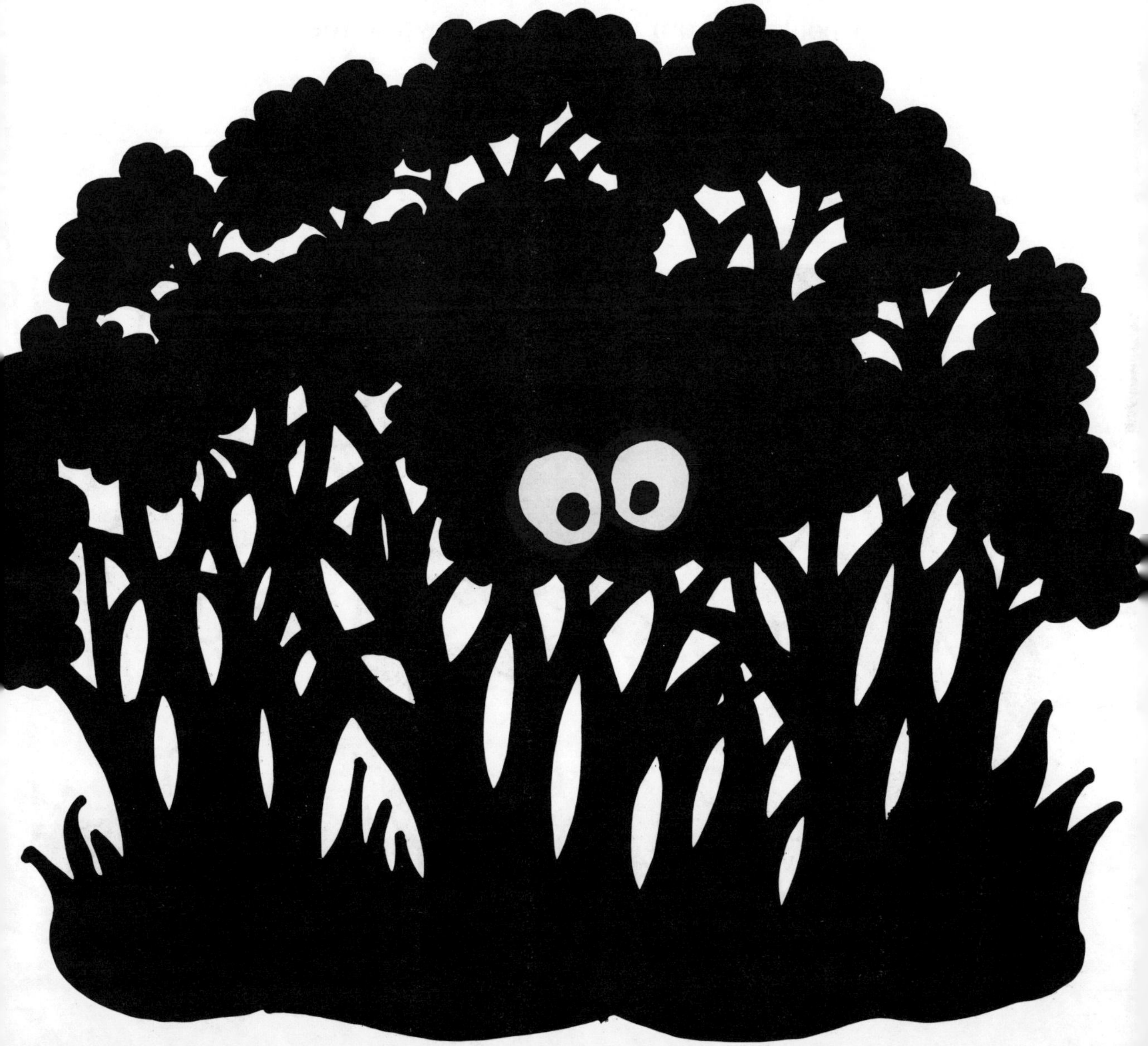

When the sun came up, they looked around
To see what had sniffled that snuffle-y sound.
Then they stamped their feet and they started to roar,
"Why it's only a sniffle-y, snuffle-y boar!"
They went back to the inn for a snack and a rest.
"Tonight," they all vowed, "is the ultimate test.
Nobody can stop us, for we're going to take
Our books and our weapons on down to the lake.

We'll cross to the island, and then we'll sit fast.
And we'll capture that terrible creature at last.
When the monster shows up, we'll be waiting and ready,
Though your bridge appears dangerous and doesn't look steady."

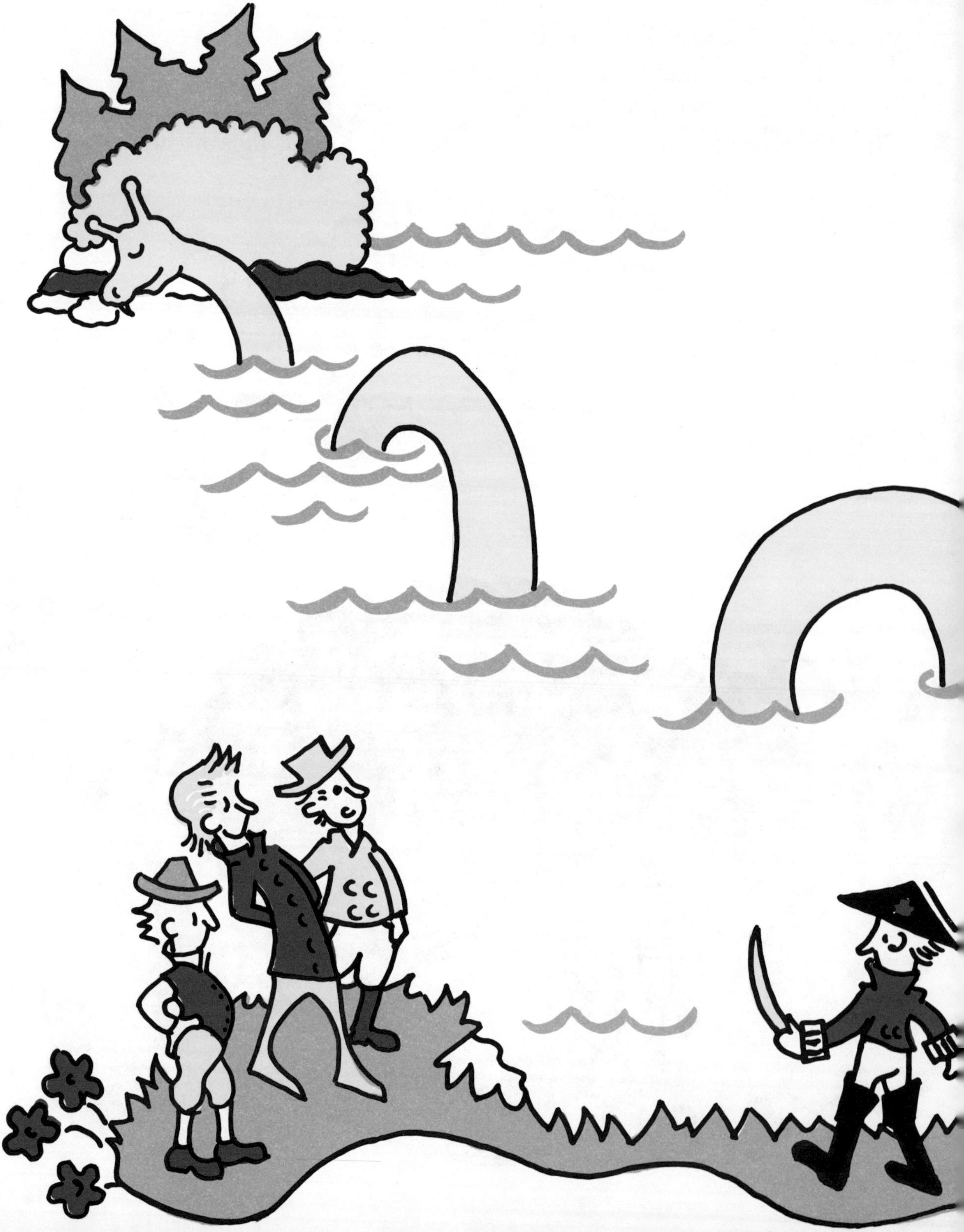

"A bridge?" thought the townsfolk. "There's been a mistake.
There isn't a bridge crossing over the lake."
(For that wasn't a bridge that the hunters had seen;
It was Phinney's long body of yellowy-green!
With his head on the island, his tail on the shore,
He was sleeping and snoring a gentle snore.)
And the townspeople murmured, "Well, this is the end;
The hunters will find that the bridge is our friend."
And they started to weep. "We have done all we could.
Our Phinney is doomed, though he's kind and he's good."

(But they never once thought, as they started to moan,
That Phinney might think of a plan of his own.)

That evening they all watched the bold hunters take
Their books and equipment along to the lake.
Each carried a weapon and lunch in a sack,
As he slithered and skidded on Phinney's slick back.

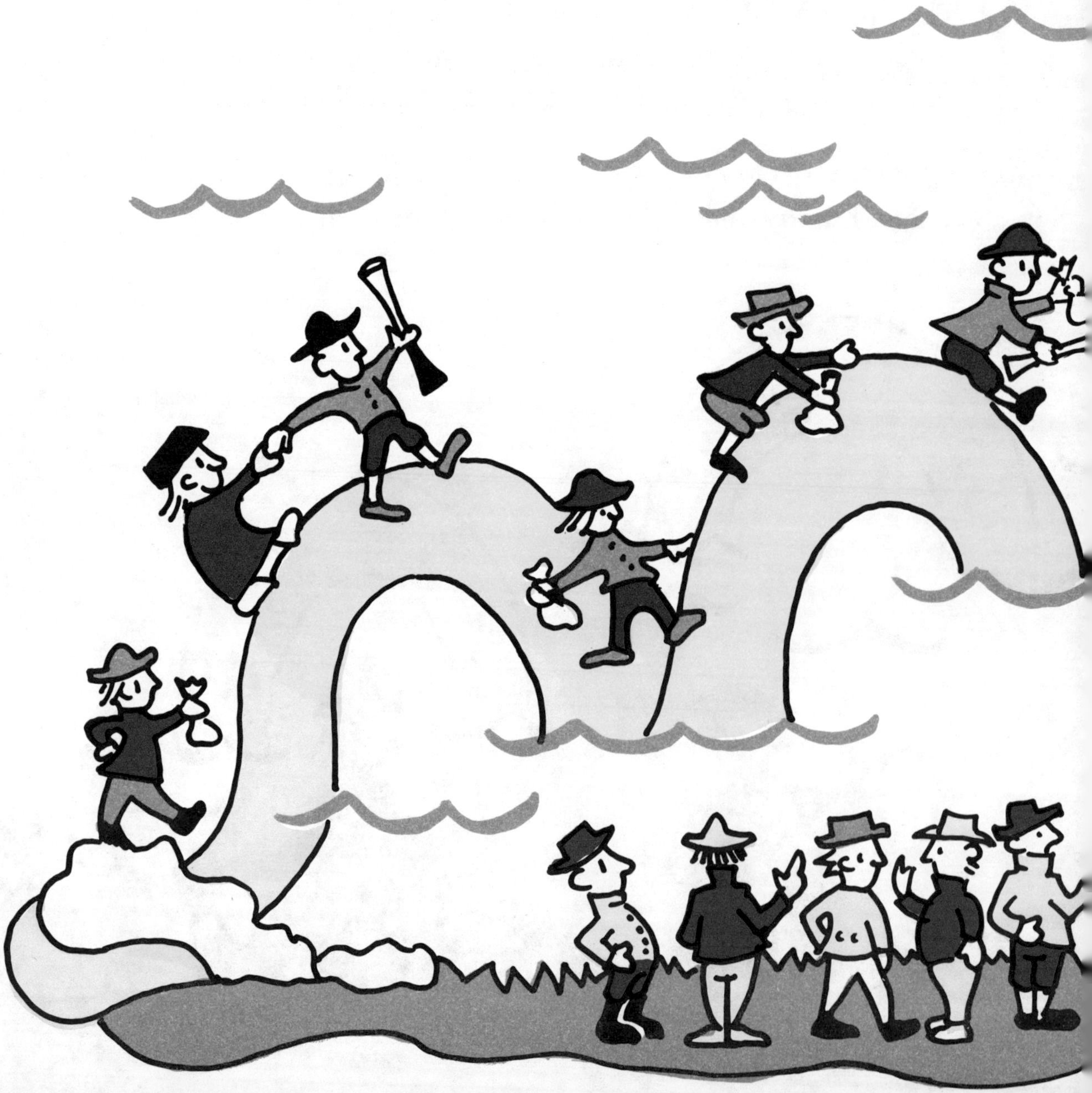

Though they whined and they muttered, "This bridge is so vile,"
The men were determined that they'd reach the isle.
They complained that the bridge was unsteady and queer,
Yet they dragged along cannon and all of their gear.

They'd slip and they'd shout, then they'd skid and they'd scream—

All the uproar awakened the beast from his dream.
When he saw what those men were attempting to do,
He decided to teach them a lesson or two.

So he smiled and he dove;
     in a moment he'd sunk,
And the soldiers and hunters went, "Whoosh!" and "Ker-Plunk!"
They flew up in the air,
        With a splash they came down—

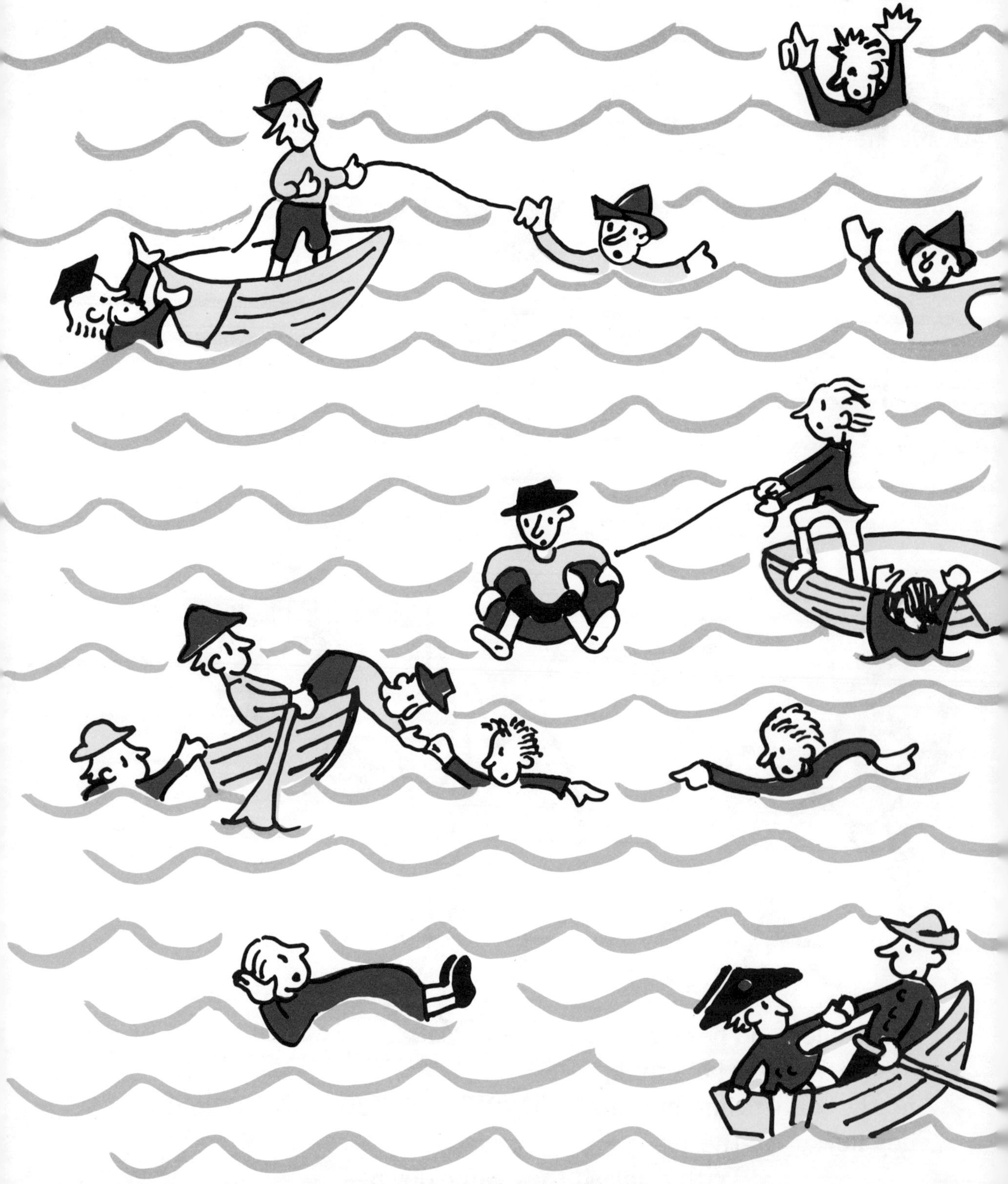

The townsfolk rushed out so the men wouldn't drown.
They rowed around saving men all through the night,
And they pulled out the last by the dawn's chilly light.
The hunters were soaked and caught colds in the head.
"The sooner we leave here, the better," they said.
"We'll never return to this miserable place.
For the monster hunt turned to a wild goose chase.
If you ever again build a bridge from this shore,
You'd better get help, or don't build any more.
That bridge was so shaky, we slipped and we slid;
We're surprised that it lasted as long as it did."
Then they all stormed away without waving good-bye;
But the townsfolk called after them, "Well, you did try.
Now you'd better report that no monster's around,
Because if there had been, he would have been found."

So the village continues to stand there today,
Hidden and secret and out-of-the-way.
No strangers venture to undertake
A journey out to that deep dark lake.
But Phinney still dives to the watery caves
Where succulent plants grow beneath the waves.
Folks tell the tale over and over again
How Phinney was saved from those arrogant men.
And people still talk of the wonderful day
When he tricked all the hunters and they ran away.